CHRISTMAS
IN THE STABLE

TEXT BY ASTRID LINDGREN

PICTURES BY HARALD WIBERG

COWARD-McCANN, INC., NEW YORK

There was a child sitting on her mother's knee who wanted to hear about Christmas. So her mother told her about Christmas in the Stable.

"There was a Christmas long ago and far away," she said, but the child did not know about long ago and far away. She knew only their own farm and a few yesterdays. And so as her mother spoke, the child saw everything as if it were happening in their own stable. Perhaps even now.

"There was an evening long ago," the mother said, "and a man and a woman were wandering along the road in the darkness."

The child nodded, picturing the road that went beside their farm.

"They had walked a long way and were tired. Now they wanted to sleep, but they did not know where to go. In all the farmhouses the lights were out. Everyone was asleep and did not care about those who wandered on the roads. It was dark and cold. There were not even any stars out to light the sky.

"But by the road there was a little stable. The man opened the door slightly and spread the light of his lantern."

The mother paused and stroked the child's hair.

"Perhaps there were animals in there," she said. "Do you think so?"

The child knew much about stables. "Yes," she agreed, "there were animals in there."

"But they were already asleep," the mother said. "When they heard someone come through the door, they woke up and saw the two wanderers standing in the light from the lantern. But why they had come to their stable in the evening, the animals did not know.

"But perhaps they could understand how cold and tired and hungry the people were. Perhaps the horse understood when the woman put her cold fingers under his mane to find the warmth there.

"Perhaps the cow understood when the woman milked her and drank her warm milk.

"Perhaps the sheep understood too, for when the woman lay down in the straw to sleep, they clustered around to give her warmth.

"So the night fell silently over the stable and all those who were in there.

"And when the night was darkest and most still, there was all at once a cry in the stable. It was the first cry of a newborn baby. At the same moment all the stars of the night came into the sky. One was bigger and brighter than the others. It took its place right over the stable and shone with a beautiful, clear light.

"Now there were shepherds out that night. They were going to fetch some sheep who were still staying in the fields, though winter had come. And the shepherds saw the star rise over the stable. They saw the whole sky lighted.

" 'Why is a star burning over our stable?' the shepherds asked each other.

" 'Come, let us go and see what has happened.'

"Along snowy paths, they hurried home with their sheep and lambs.

"In the stable they found a newborn child lying in his mother's arms.

" 'The star is shining because of the child,' the shepherds whispered. 'Never before was there a child born in our stable.'

"Now the child needed sleep, but there was neither cradle nor bed. Only a crib was there with hay in it for the horse to eat. The mother made a soft, hollow place in the hay and laid her child down. The horse stood still, his eyes gentle, as he watched.

"So the night passed. The child slept in the crib. The animals and shepherds stood silently around. Everything was quiet.

"Over the stable the Christmas star kept shining. For it was on a Christmas night that all this happened. A Christmas night long ago and far away. The very first one."

The child looked up at her mother and smiled. She did not know about long ago and far away. But now she knew about Christmas.

LCC: 62-14449   ISBN 0-698-20677-0
1 3 5 7 9 10 8 6 4 2
First Sandcastle Books edition